Shadow
in Trouble

Enid Blyton

Illustrated by Rowan Clifford

CARNIVAL

Shadow the sheepdog had learnt many things from the other dogs on the farm. Dandy, Tinker, Rafe and Bob taught him how to round up sheep, how to take them where they should go, and how to guide them home when they were lost.

But the shepherd would not let Shadow do very much alone with the sheep, though the puppy longed to show the other dogs how clever he was.

"Oh, why can't I round up the sheep by myself?" yelped Shadow one morning. "I know exactly what to do. I could round up all this flock and take them to the next field by myself – but Bob won't let me, and the shepherd won't either."

"Be patient," said Tinker. "You may think you know a lot, but you don't. You couldn't possibly take these sheep into the next field by yourself."

But Shadow was cross, and he watched for a chance to show Johnny and the other dogs just how clever he was!

One afternoon, Shadow noticed a small flock of sheep up on the hillside, quite away from the others.

"Just look at that!" wuffed Shadow to himself. "Those sheep have got away! The other dogs haven't noticed. I wonder where they are."

He went to see. Dandy was nowhere to be seen.
Bob was lying down in the shade of the
shepherd's hut, near his master, one eye open,
and one ear cocked. He growled when he saw
Shadow, and the puppy hurriedly ran away.

Tinker was scraping madly at a big rabbit-
hole and paid no attention at all to Shadow.
Rafe was lying asleep in the warm sun.

"Well, look at that now!" said Shadow to
himself, puzzled. "Sheep have escaped from the
flock and have taken themselves up there. They
may get quite lost. And none of the dogs has
noticed!"

He stood and looked at Rafe, wondering if he should wake him. Then a great thought came into his head.

"Bones and biscuits! Here's a chance for me to show what I can do! *I'll* get those sheep down from that field up there myself – and take them to the others!"

As soon as he thought of this, Shadow was running as fast as he could over the green hillside to where the little group of sheep grazed peacefully in a field way above the other sheep.

"Now let me think first," said Shadow, as he leapt through the gate. "The sheep are all over there – I must think how I am to take them out of the field. I wonder if there is a gap anywhere?"

Shadow ran round the hedges. At the top of the field he found a small gap. He thought it must be the one that the sheep had found to get into the field.

"Good!" he said. "Now I'll bunch them together and drive them to the gap."

He ran over to the sheep. They looked surprised to see him, but went on eating the grass. Shadow remembered that it was better not to bark too much in case he frightened them.

So he ran first at one sheep and then at another, and soon one big sheep began to run up the field. The others followed. Shadow ran after the first sheep and headed it towards the gap. The sheep did not see it and ran right past.

Shadow felt angry. He tried to make another sheep go through the gap. "Get back, sheep, get back. Can't you see the hole in the hedge?"

At last one sheep did see it and managed to squeeze through in a great fright. Another followed and another – but the rest ran excitedly round the field and simply would *not* go through the gap!

At last the puppy lay down on the grass, tired out. It was no good! He couldn't get all the sheep out!

"But, tails and whiskers – where did those sheep go that *did* get out?" suddenly wondered the puppy. "I'd better go and look!"

He jumped through the gap and began to hunt for the three sheep. They all seemed to have gone different ways! He put his nose to the ground and sniffed. Yes – one had gone this way – one that way – and the third one another way.

He set off after the first sheep, his nose to the ground. The sheep had gone right to the top of the hill – and over the other side!

He tore up the hill and down the other side. He suddenly saw the sheep peacefully pulling at some rich green grass in a ditch.

"Come back, silly, come back!" barked Shadow. "You are going the wrong way! Oh, do come back. I've got the others to find too!"

But the sheep was too frightened to go back,
even though Shadow got ahead of her and tried
to turn her. She trotted on and on, and the
puppy grew frightened.

"What shall I do? I'd better go back and get
one of the other dogs," thought the puppy.
"Bones and biscuits! Why did I ever try to do
this by myself?"

He turned round and ran back up the hillside.
Over the top he went, round the hedge, and
scampered to where he had left Tinker and Rafe.
Tinker was sitting looking rather puzzled, and
Rafe was awake now and standing with his ears
cocked. Both dogs knew that something was
wrong. Bob was growling behind the shepherd's
hut.

"Now what's the matter, young pup?" barked
Rafe. "What have you been doing?"

"I've been trying my best to get all those sheep in that little field back to the big field," yelped Shadow. "I am surprised that none of you noticed they had got away from the flock."

Bob came trotting up, his ears well back. He came right up to Shadow.

"Let me tell you that I had orders from my master this morning to separate those sheep from the others," he said. "That is why they are there. Do you suppose that we should not have noticed something wrong if we hadn't known they were meant to be up there?"

"Oh," wuffed poor Shadow, feeling very silly all at once. "I'm sorry, Bob – but I've tried to get them back to the others – and three got through a gap in the hedge – and . . ."

The three dogs stared at Shadow in horror.

"What!" cried Rafe, "you got three out? Where are they? Did you get them safely back to the flock? What happened?"

"I don't know what happened to two of them," yelped Shadow, his tail drooping sadly. "I followed the third and couldn't get it back. It is on the other side of the hill. I came to get your help."

Without losing a moment Bob barked some orders to the other two, and they all set off at a gallop.

Bob ran down the hill, Rafe ran another way, and Tinker went bounding over a rocky piece of ground to find one of the lost sheep.

Poor little Shadow did not join in at all. He sat down, his ears drooping, and his pink tongue hanging out. He was very miserable indeed.

"I'm not so clever as I thought I was," he yelped sadly. "What will the other dogs say to me when they get back?"

The more he thought about that, the less he liked the idea. And at last he got up and began to creep down the hill towards the farm.

On the way he met Dandy, who was coming back from a long walk all by himself.

"What's up, young pup?" asked the big sheepdog in surprise, for he saw that Shadow's tail was well between his legs, curled up under his tummy.

Shadow told him everything. "So you see I'm in disgrace," he wuffed sadly. "And I'm just going back to the farm to Johnny, before Tinker, Rafe, and Bob come back and say horrid things to me."

"Well, if you take my advice, you'll stay up here on the hill and hear what they've got to say," said Dandy at once. "No good ever comes of running away from trouble, young pup. Be brave, can't you?"

Shadow stood and thought, his tail drooping. Then he turned back up the hill.

"You're right, Dandy," he said. "I mustn't run away from trouble. After all, it was my own fault, and I must put up with it."

"Good for you, young pup," said Dandy. "I'll come along with you."

Bob, Rafe, and Tinker had found the three sheep and were making them go through the gap in the hedge by the time that Dandy and Shadow reached them.

"One of us must stay here whilst the shepherd is fetched to mend this gap," said Bob. "Once a sheep knows a hole it will keep getting out of it, and maybe the others will follow. You are silly as a sheep, Shadow! This little crowd of sheep were brought up here, and put in through the gate – and you go and show them a hole to escape from! You'll never be any good!"

"Why couldn't you tell us if you thought
anything was wrong?" asked Rafe angrily.
"I suppose you think you're so clever that you
can do things on your own! Stupid young pup!"

Poor Shadow was very upset and miserable.
He put his tail between his legs and began to
creep away down the hillside. Then Dandy
spoke up for him.

"Well, he may be a very silly little pup, but at
least he did stay to get his scolding," he said.
"He was running away when I met him – but he
came back to hear what you all had to say.
He is at least brave, Bob."

The three dogs said nothing for a minute. Then Rafe called after Shadow. "You can come up to us tomorrow if you like, and we'll show you how to get back a wandering sheep. But don't you dare to do anything on your own again till we tell you that you're grown-up!"

So Shadow felt a little happier as he ran slowly back to the farm. "That was a hard lesson to learn," thought the little puppy, "but I'm jolly glad I wasn't afraid to learn it!"